peg + cat

The Race Car Problem

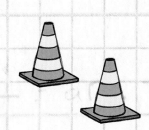

JENNIFER OXLEY
+ BILLY ARONSON

WALKER
ENTERTAINMENT

One day Peg and Cat
went to the junkyard.
On a normal day,
they wouldn't have
much use for a bunch
of old junk.

But this was not a normal day.
It was the day of the
Tallapegga Twenty—
a really big-deal race!
Peg and Cat had come to
the junkyard to build...

2+1=3

a race car!

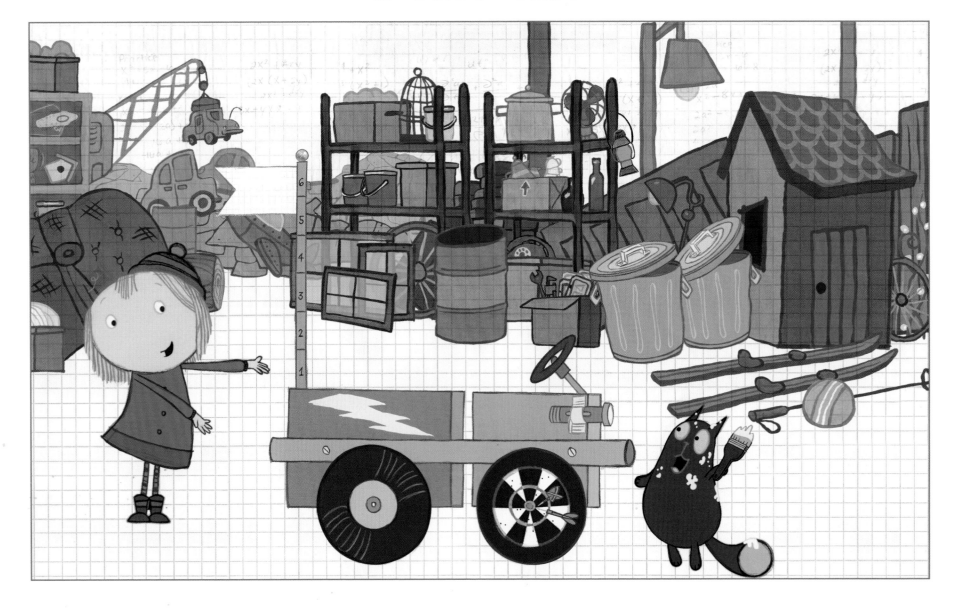

They called it ***Hot-Buttered Lightning***,
because they hoped it would be as swift as a bolt of lightning.
(They added "hot-buttered" to make the name even better,
the way butter makes popcorn even better.)

3+1=4

Hot-Buttered Lightning was made of boxes held together by a long metal cylinder. It had four round things for wheels.

"She's a sweet ride," said Cat.
"The other cars don't stand a chance!"

"Ready to race, Cat?" asked Peg.

"I was born ready," he answered.

"Then buckle up and let's roll!"

Hot-Buttered Lightning rolled-
sort of.

BOUNCE, BOUNCE, BOING! SCREEEEEECH!

4+1=5

"We lost a wheel!" said Peg.

"One new wheel, coming right up," said Cat,
grabbing the nearest piece of junk
and putting it on the car.

CRASH-BANG! CRASH-BANG!

"The new wheel is a square," said Peg.
"A wheel has to be round to roll.
WE'VE GOT A BIG PROBLEM!
Uh ... Cat?" Peg called.
"Where'd you go?"

"Over here!" said Cat, peeking out of
a bin with a lid on his head.
(Cat was always tripping
and falling into things.)

"That's it,
you junk-wearing genius!"
said Peg.
"That bin lid is ROUND.
It'll be a perfect wheel!
PROBLEM SOLVED!"

6+1=7

At the racetrack, referee
Ramone welcomed the crowd.
"Ladies and gentlemen,
let's meet the racers!"

"Here come the Pirates,
in their Pirate Mobile.
Part car and part boat,
this fearsome race car
is fast on land and sea!"

"ARRRRRR,"
growled the Pirates.

7+1=8

"Next up are the Teens in
their awesome Pizza Mobile!
Fuelled by crisps
and cherry cola,
it's one hot slice of speed!"

"Woot, woot!"
yelped the Teens.

"And here comes our next racer!
In his sleek, jet-powered
Triangle Mobile,
it's the Pig!"

The Pig waved to his fans
and snorted.

8+1=9

"And finally,
here are Peg and Cat in
Hot-Buttered Lightning,
their race car made out of rubbish!"

"The other cars are so much
bigger than ours!" said Peg.

"And so much cooler," said Cat.

"We've got a

REALLY BIG PROBLEM!"
said Peg.
"There's no way we can win the race.
Maybe we should just give up."

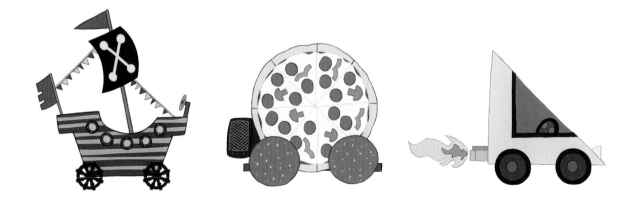

"Did someone say give up?"
asked Ramone. "You never solve
a problem by giving up. Keep trying
your hardest, no matter what.
And you just might win
the golden cup!"

"The golden cup!" gasped Cat.
"Whoa-ho-ho-ho-ho-ho!" (Those 5 "hos"
tied Cat's record for most "hos" he
had ever said after a "whoa"!)

"We won't give up, Ramone,"
said Peg. "Thanks for totally inspiring us!"

"I do what I can," he answered.

Then Ramone explained the rules
to the racers. "When you go all the way
around the track, that's called a lap.
The first car to drive 20 laps wins!

So ... gentlemen, ladies, parrots, swine-
start your engines!
On your mark, get set ... GO!"

11+1=12

"And
they're off!"
said Connie.

Neighbour Ladies
Connie and Viv were
the announcers.

13+1=14

"The Pig, in his Triangle Mobile, takes an early lead!"
said Viv. "But the Pizza Mobile isn't far behind.
The Pirates are right behind the Teens.
And there are Peg and Cat, bringing up the rear."

"Whose rear are we bringing up?" asked Cat.

"Bringing up the rear means we're behind everyone else,"
Peg explained.

14+1=15

When Peg and Cat made it
all the way around the track,
Ramone put a big number 1 on their car.

"We finished one whole lap,"
said Cat. "We are GOOD!"

"But the Pirate Mobile has a 4," said Peg.
"And the Pizza Mobile has a 6!
We know that 4 is more than 1.
And 6 is even more than 4.
So they've done more laps
than we have."

"We'll never win!"
said Cat.

"Remember what Ramone said?"
Peg asked.

"Something about giving up..."

"He said not to!" Peg said
as they kept on chugging ahead.

6 > 4 > 1

6
5
4
3
2
1

16+1=17

"The Pig is slowing down,"
Connie announced,
"to eat a piece of pie...
shaped like a triangle!"

The Pirates were slowing down
for a snack, too.

"Give me that peach!"
yelled Captain.

"It's mine!" shouted Buckler.

"I got squirted with peach juice!"
said Grey Beard.

"Serves ye right fer squeezin'
me peach!" said Matey.

17+1=18

"Look at the Teens!"
Viv said.
"They're eating their car!"

Viv was right.
The Teens had stopped
to eat tasty slices
of the Pizza Mobile!

But not everyone
was stopping for a snack.

"Little Peggy and her Cat friend
are still rolling right along!"
announced Connie.

When the Teens completed their next lap,
Ramone put a 13 on their car.

"We made it into the teens!" shouted Mora.
"WOO, like, HOOO!"

Suddenly Jesse stopped the Pizza Mobile.
"If we keep driving, we'll get to

Then we'll drive out of the teens."

"Let's keep this teen number
on our car forEVER!" said Tessa.

The other Teens agreed.
So they drove the Pizza Mobile
right off the track
and out of the race.

20+1=21

Soon Peg and Cat had
completed 15 laps.

"We're ahead of the Pirates,
right?" asked Cat.

"The Pirates have 18,"
Peg explained. "And just as
8 is more than 5,
18 is more than 15."

18 > 15

"So we're not ahead
of the Pirates,"
Cat said.

"You're learning!"
said Peg.

"Learning and losing,"
said Cat.

The Pirates were arguing again.

"Let me steer!"
said Captain.

"It's my turn to drive!"
said Buckler.

"Don't be a baby!" said Matey.

"Waaaa!" said Grey Beard.

All four Pirates
grabbed at the wheel,
until **POP!**
it came flying off.
The Pirate Mobile went
swerving off the track
and into a lake.

22+1=23

With the Pirates out of the race,
it was down to just two cars:
the Triangle Mobile and *Hot-Buttered Lightning*.

But suddenly Peg and Cat's car hit a bump - and **THUD!**
The long metal pipe snapped in half.
Without the pipe to hold it together,
Hot-Buttered Lightning fell apart.

"I am TOTALLY FREAKING OUT!"
said Peg.

Cat put up his paws
and gave Peg a look.

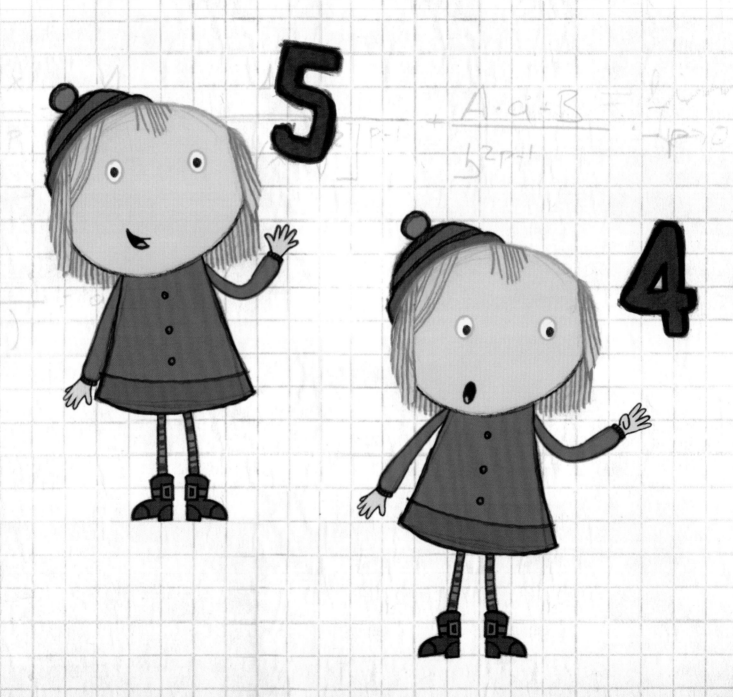

26+1=27

As Peg counted,
Cat glanced at the
parrot's telescope.

"That's it, you genius
Cat!" said Peg,
giving Cat a big squishy hug.
"That telescope is a cylinder!
It's a tube with circles on its ends,
just like the long metal pipe.
So we can use it to hold

Hot-Buttered Lightning

together!"

When Peg and Cat
replaced the broken pipe
with the telescope,
their car was back
in action.

But the Pig was still ahead.
Having finished
19 laps, he was about
to finish lap number 20
and win the race...

Suddenly, the
Triangle Mobile
screeched to a halt.

"What's going on?"
asked Connie.

"The Teens and Pirates
are getting their
consolation prizes,"
Viv explained,
"racing flags shaped
like triangles."

"Ohhhhh!" Connie said.
"And the Pig
loves triangles!"

In a burst of passion,
the Pig leapt out
of his car and
into the stands.
He had left the race
to surround himself
with triangles!

Now there was only one car still in the race.
One little rickety car made out of junk.

Peg and Cat finished lap 19 and kept right on going.
And in no time, they were sputtering towards the end of lap 20.

"PEG AND CAT ARE CROSSING THE FINISH LINE!"
yelled Viv.

"THEY WON THE RACE!" screamed Connie.

"YAAAAAAYYYYY!" cheered the crowd.

"You were right," Peg said to Ramone
as he put a 20 on *Hot-Buttered Lightning*.
"We didn't give up. We kept right on going no matter what.
And we won the race!"

Ramone presented Peg and Cat with their prize:
the golden cup.

"WHOA-HO-HO-HO-HO-HO-HO!" (A record-breaking 6 "hos"!)

"PROBLEM SOLVED!" said Peg.

29+1=30

30+1=31

This book is based on the TV series Peg + Cat.
Peg + Cat is produced by The Fred Rogers Company.
Created by Jennifer Oxley and Billy Aronson.
The Race Car Problem is based on a television script by Kevin Del Aguila
and background art by Amy DeLay.
The PBS KIDS logo is a registered mark of the Public Broadcasting Service
and is used with permission.

First published 2015 by Walker Entertainment,
an imprint of Walker Books Ltd
87 Vauxhall Walk, London SE11 5HJ

2 4 6 8 10 9 7 5 3 1

Copyright © 2015 by Feline Features, LLC

Printed in Humen, Dongguan, China

This book has been typeset in OPTITypewriter.
The illustrations were created digitally.

British Library Cataloguing in Publication Data:
a catalogue record for this book is available
from the British Library

ISBN 978-1-4063-6611-2
www.walker.co.uk

8

7

6

5

4

3

2

1